The ... ouse,
The Red Ripe Strawberry, and
THE BI... Y BEAR

by Don and Audrey ... strated by Don Wood

Published by Child's Play (International) Ltd

This impression 1997/3
ISBN 0-85953-182-1 (hard cover)
ISBN 0-85953-012-4 (soft cover)
Printed in Singapore
Library of Congress Number 90-46414
A catalogue reference for this book is available from the British Library

Hello, little Mouse.
What are you doing?

Oh, I see.

Are you going to pick
that red, ripe strawberry?

But, little Mouse,
haven't you heard
about the big,
hungry Bear?

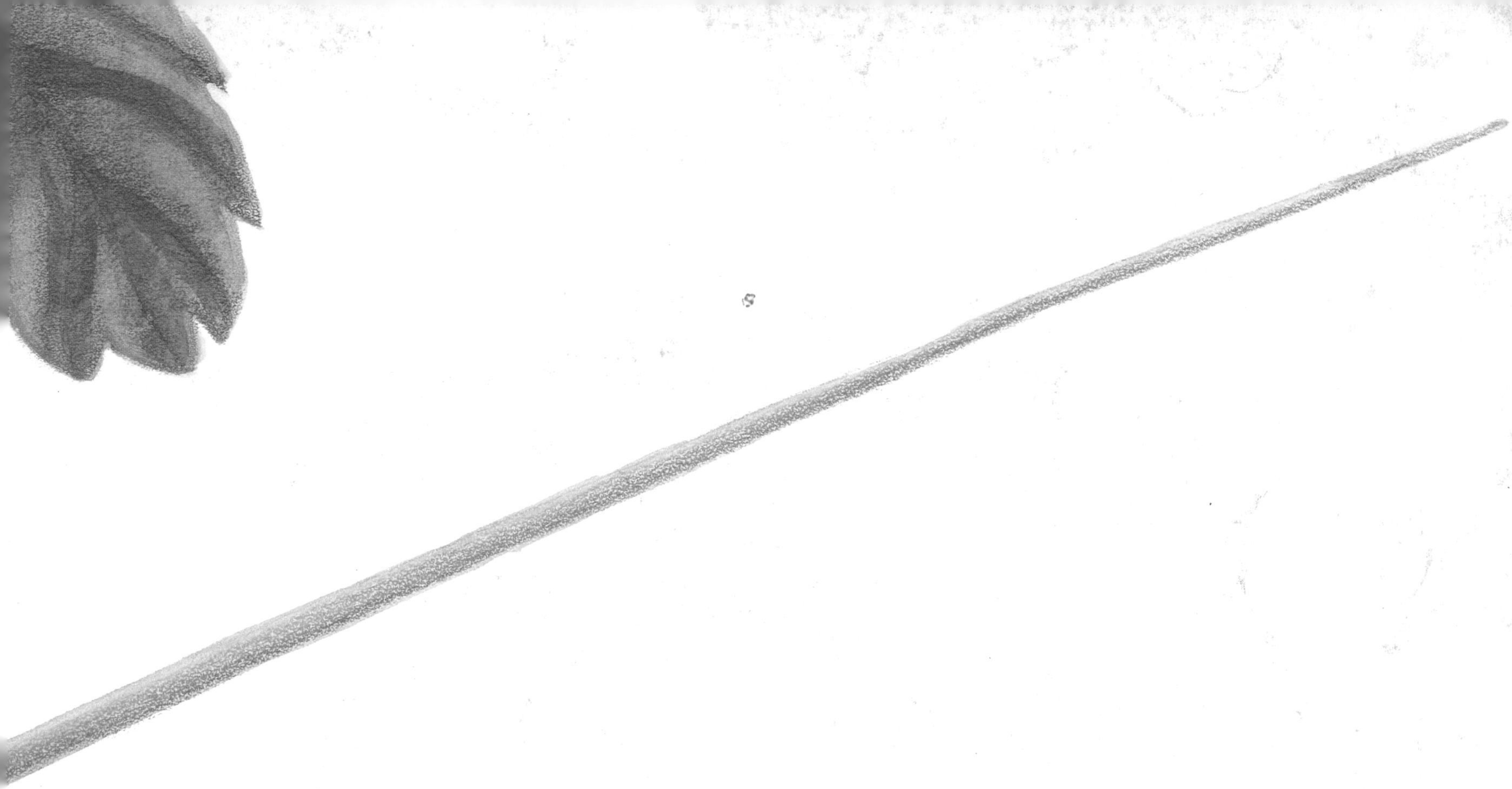

Ohhh, how that Bear
loves red, ripe strawberries!

The big, hungry Bear
can smell a red, ripe
strawberry a mile away . . .

Especially, one that has
just been picked.

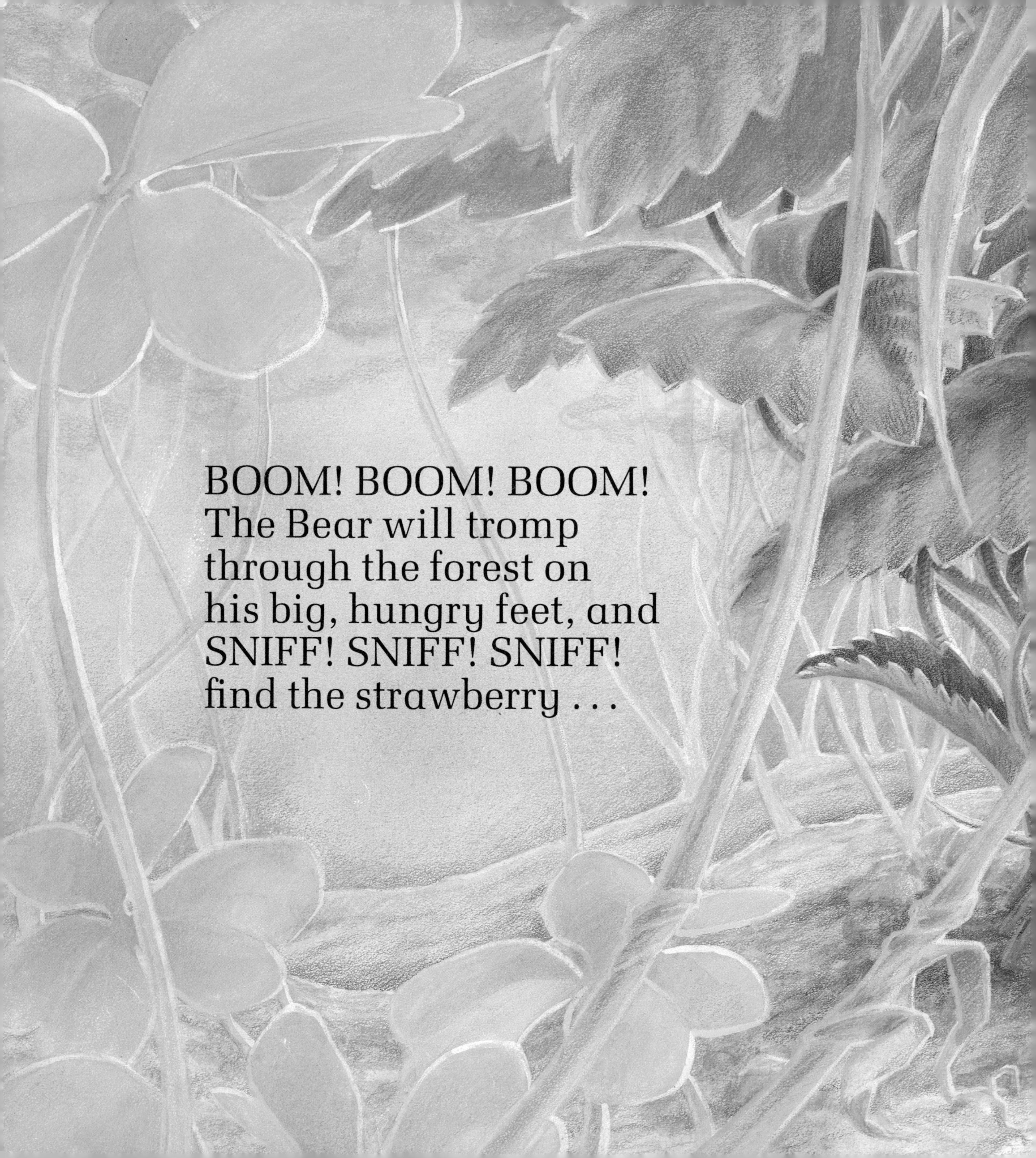

BOOM! BOOM! BOOM!
The Bear will tromp
through the forest on
his big, hungry feet, and
SNIFF! SNIFF! SNIFF!
find the strawberry . . .

No matter where
it is hidden,

or who is guarding it,

or how it is disguised.

Quick! There's only one way
in the whole wide world to save
a red, ripe strawberry from
the big, hungry Bear!

Cut it in two.

Share half with me.

And we'll both eat it
all up. YUM!

Now, that's one red, ripe
strawberry the big, hungry
Bear will never get!

The End